Sabrina Sue
Loves the City

written and illustrated by
Priscilla Burris

Ready-to-Read

Simon Spotlight
New York   London   Toronto   Sydney   New Delhi

For Christina Tugeau and Christy Ewers

SIMON SPOTLIGHT
An imprint of Simon & Schuster Children's Publishing Division
1230 Avenue of the Americas, New York, New York 10020
This Simon Spotlight edition December 2021
Copyright © 2021 by Priscilla Burris
SIMON SPOTLIGHT, READY-TO-READ, and colophon are registered
trademarks of Simon & Schuster, Inc.
For information about special discounts for bulk purchases, please contact
Simon & Schuster Special Sales at 1-866-506-1949
or business@simonandschuster.com.
Manufactured in the United States of America 1121 LAK
2 4 6 8 10 9 7 5 3 1
Library of Congress Cataloging-in-Publication Data
Names: Burris, Priscilla, author, illustrator.
Title: Sabrina Sue loves the city / written and illustrated by Priscilla Burris.
Description: Simon Spotlight edition. | New York : Simon Spotlight, 2022. | Series:
Sabrina Sue | Summary: Little chicken Sabrina Sue sets off on an adventure to the
big city where she hopes to see tall buildings, taxicabs, museums, and more.
Identifiers: LCCN 2021032907 (print) | LCCN 2021032908 (ebook) |
ISBN 9781665900386 (hardcover) | ISBN 9781665900379 (paperback) |
ISBN 9781665900393 (ebook) | Subjects: CYAC: Chickens—Fiction. |
Cities and towns—Fiction. Classification: LCC PZ7.B94065 Sad 2022 (print) |
LCC PZ7.B94065 (ebook) | DDC [E]—dc23
LC record available at https://lccn.loc.gov/2021032907
LC ebook record available at https://lccn.loc.gov/2021032908

Sabrina Sue lived on a farm.

Sometimes when it was
too quiet,

she thought about the city.

She asked her farm friends.

She wondered about it.
She sang about it.

Her farm friends spoke to her.

Sabrina Sue liked being busy and going far away sometimes.

Should she not go?

She thought about what to do.

She made a plan and packed for her trip.

One night she slept in
Farmer Martha's truck,
ready to go.

They rumbled up over hills.

They honked through a dark tunnel.

They turned right, and they turned left.

Farmer Martha's truck
slowed down.

Will I ever see the city?
Sabrina Sue wondered.

Sabrina Sue hopped down.
She checked her plan.

She followed the signs and walked and walked.

She looked up high and saw—the city!

It was so tall!

There is so much to see!

There is so much to do!

Sabrina Sue loved being in the city.

She wished her farm
friends were with her.
She missed them.

Sabrina Sue was happy to be back on the farm.

But someday she would visit the city again!